D1123790

Visit us on the Web!
Seussville.com
rhcbooks.com

Educators and librarians, for a variety of teaching tools, visit us at RHTeachersLibrarians.com

Library of Congress Cataloging-in-Publication Data is available upon request.
ISBN 978-0-593-18146-1 (trade) — ISBN 978-0-593-18147-8 (lib. bdg.)

MANUFACTURED IN CHINA
10 9 8 7 6 5 4 3 2
First Edition

IF I RAN YOUR SCHOOL

by **the Cat in the Hat**
with a little help from **Alastair Heim**

illustrated by **Tom Brannon**

WITHDRAWN

BEGINNER BOOKS ®
A Division of Random House

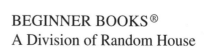

I just heard a thing
so I came right away!
The KING of all unfunny
things, I must say . . .

I heard that you two—
or, perhaps, maybe YOU—
think going to school
is a DULL thing to do.
I came here to show you
that school can be FUN!
I showed up to show you
how school fun is DONE.

If I ran your school,
we would start every day
in a PLEDGE-FULLY way
as we stand up and say . . .

"Today I will learn
how much fun FUN can be!
From eight after eight
until three after three,
I will smile all the while
with a grin on my chin
till the end of the day
from the time we begin!"

If I ran your school,
we would get a class pet.
But not just ONE pet . . .
ALL the pets we can get!

Some would be FUZZY
and some would be WET,
and others would come
as a TWO-FOR-ONE set.

If I ran your school,
I would help you to read
by giving each student
a BOOK-BLOOMING SEED.

Each seed would be planted
and grown in a pot.
And after we water
and water A LOT . . .

... the seeds would sprout BOOKS
that would fill up the room!
The more that you read them,
the more YOU would bloom!

If I ran your school,
I would give a POP QUIZ
where we take and we shake
every bottle there is
until they EXPLODE
into fountains of FIZZ.

$2 + 3 = 5$

$2 + 2 = 4$

$1 + 2 = 3$

$2 + 3 = 6$

And IF you can guess
how much FIZZ that there is,
it TRULY would make you
a POP FIZZ QUIZ WHIZ!

If I ran your school,
on the days you have art,
I would drive all around
in my ART-MAKING CART.

My CART-TO-MAKE-ART
would have glitter and glue
and LOTS of fun things
that are perfect for you.

At twelve after twelve,
we would serve a buffet
of pizzas and pancakes
and tray after tray
of berries and cherries
and swirly sorbet
to keep you well fed
for the rest of the day.

If I ran your school,
we would cover your sneakers
in DOUBLE-BOUNCE BUBBLES
we brew in these beakers
to give your old sneakers
a little more pep . . .

If I ran your school,
we would play a FUN song.
While I waved this wood wand
and you all played along . . .

The DRUMMERS and FLUTERS
and TUBA TOOT-TOOTERS,
and ALL of the players
with sliding trombones
and THREE-NOZZLED BLOOZERS
and SAX-A-MA-PHONES,
would take their tune makers
and turn them around
and play them all BACKWARD.
Just THINK of the sound!

If I ran your school,
we would have SMELL-AND-TELL,
where you bring in a thing
(and that thing has a smell).

We would smell that thing well
as you stand up and tell
how the thing that you bring
got its good or bad smell.

If I ran your school,
I would sit in the bleachers
and cheer you all on,
right along with your teachers,
through round after round
after round after round
of SCHOOL-A-HOOP HOOPLA
to see who gets crowned . . .

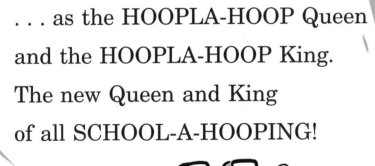

. . . as the HOOPLA-HOOP Queen
and the HOOPLA-HOOP King.
The new Queen and King
of all SCHOOL-A-HOOPING!

If I ran your school,
at your very last class,
you ALL would be getting
a GO WILD PASS!

Your classes are over!
Your school day is done!
And NOW it is time
for some fun in the sun!

LITTLE CAT FAIR

School

Then ALL of my Little Cat
crew would be there
to welcome you all
to their LITTLE CAT FAIR!
The games and the rides
and the LOOP-THE-LOOP slides
and the EXTRA-fun prizes
that come in all sizes
should keep you all smiling
the whole school year through . . .

If I ran your school,
THAT is what I would do,
then tip my top hat and say
"FAIR-WELL" to you!
There MAY be more schools
that will need me, you see,
to show them how FUN
that THEIR school day can be . . .

Do YOU think your school
needs a visit from me?

31901067816894